**Based on characters created
by Jean and Laurent de Brunhoff**
Based on a story by J.D. Smith
Image adaptation by Van Gool-Lefèvre-Loiseaux
Produced by Twin Books U.K. Ltd, London

This 1990 edition published by JellyBean Press,
distributed by Outlet Book Company, Inc.,
a Random House Company,
225 Park Avenue South
New York NY 10003

ISBN 0-517-051966

8 7 6 5 4 3 2 1

Printed and bound in Barcelona, Spain by Cronion, S.A.

DEP. LEG. B-32.548-90

BABAR

The Phantom

JellyBean Press
New York

Pom and Flora were practicing the piano. Actually, Flora was practicing. Pom was just hitting the keys. Flora wanted to show her brother how to play a scale, but he answered, "No, I don't need any help. I can do it myself. Do, mi, re, fa . . ."

"Pom," said Babar, "one can always use a helping hand, especially when one is young. I learned this myself when I was only a little older than you, from the Phantom of the Opera."

Sitting down at the piano, Babar played a pretty little melody and began his story. . . .

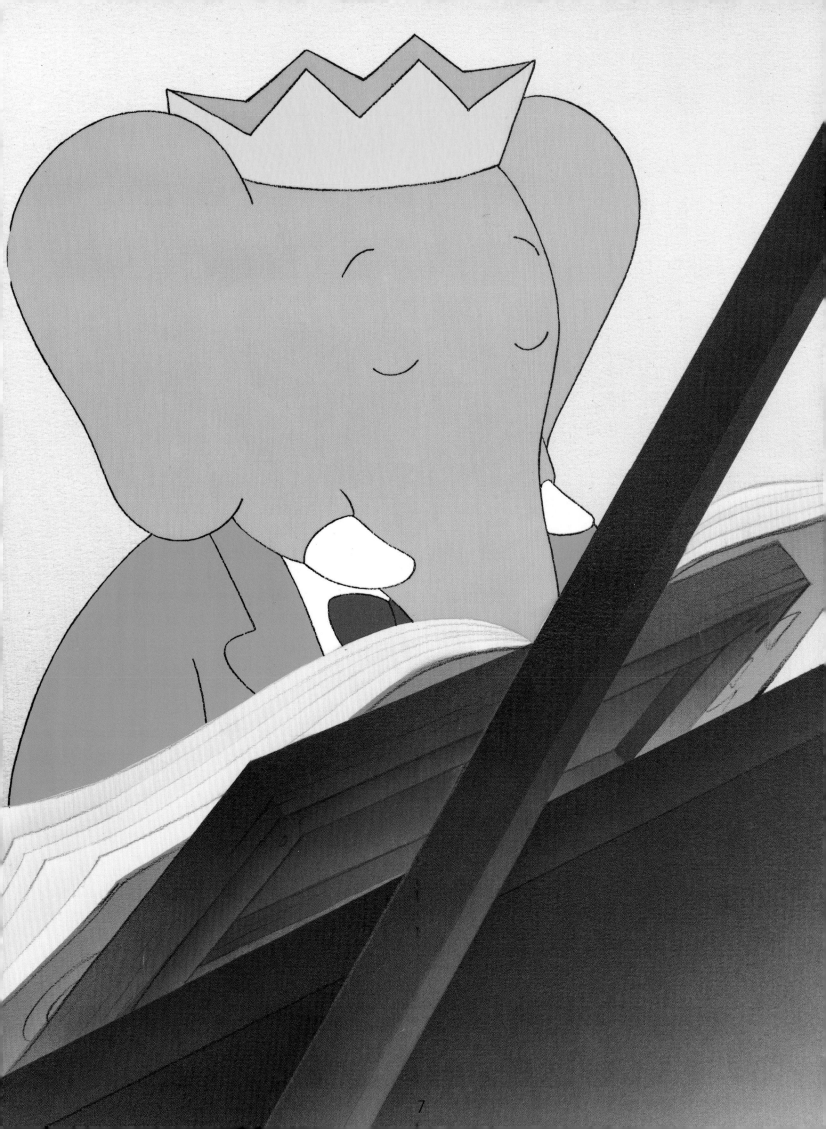

One evening Babar was walking home
from school with several of his friends.
"Let's go this way," said the little elephant.
"Oh, no!" they cried. "That takes you past
the old opera house, and it's haunted." And
they ran away as fast as they could.

Babar was still quite young, but he was no coward. "I don't believe in ghosts," he said. And to prove it, he walked close to the old building, which had been deserted for many years. Suddenly, he heard something. There was music, a real concert, coming from inside the deserted opera house.

No elephant had ever moved so fast. Babar was sure that the strange musician was a ghost, and he ran as quickly as his little legs could carry him. He felt better when he saw his own house at the end of the street, but he didn't stop running.

He ran right upstairs, and in spite of his little round tum, he managed to wiggle under the bed. Suddenly, the door opened . . .

. . . and his dear friend and adoptive mother, the Old Lady, came into the room.

"Why, Babar, what has happened?"

"The ghost. I heard the ghost at the opera."

"A ghost? But such things don't exist," she said gently. "Come on, now, you big silly. Give me a hug and tell me all about it while you get ready for bed."

Perhaps the Old Lady was right! Perhaps ghosts didn't exist. But Babar thought about it all the next day, and the beautiful melody he had heard kept running through his head. Who had been playing it? He decided to find out.

That evening, Babar went back to the old opera house. He listened very carefully, but could hear nothing. Silence had taken the place of the music he had heard the night before. Babar knew he hadn't imagined the whole thing, so he decided to find a way into the old building and take a closer look.

When Babar had slipped under the boards nailed across the broken doors, and crossed the dusty and rubble-strewn lobby, he heard the music again. He made his way into the auditorium, and the music grew louder. Despite his terror, he could make out a figure seated at the keyboard of the opera house's pipe organ. It was the phantom!

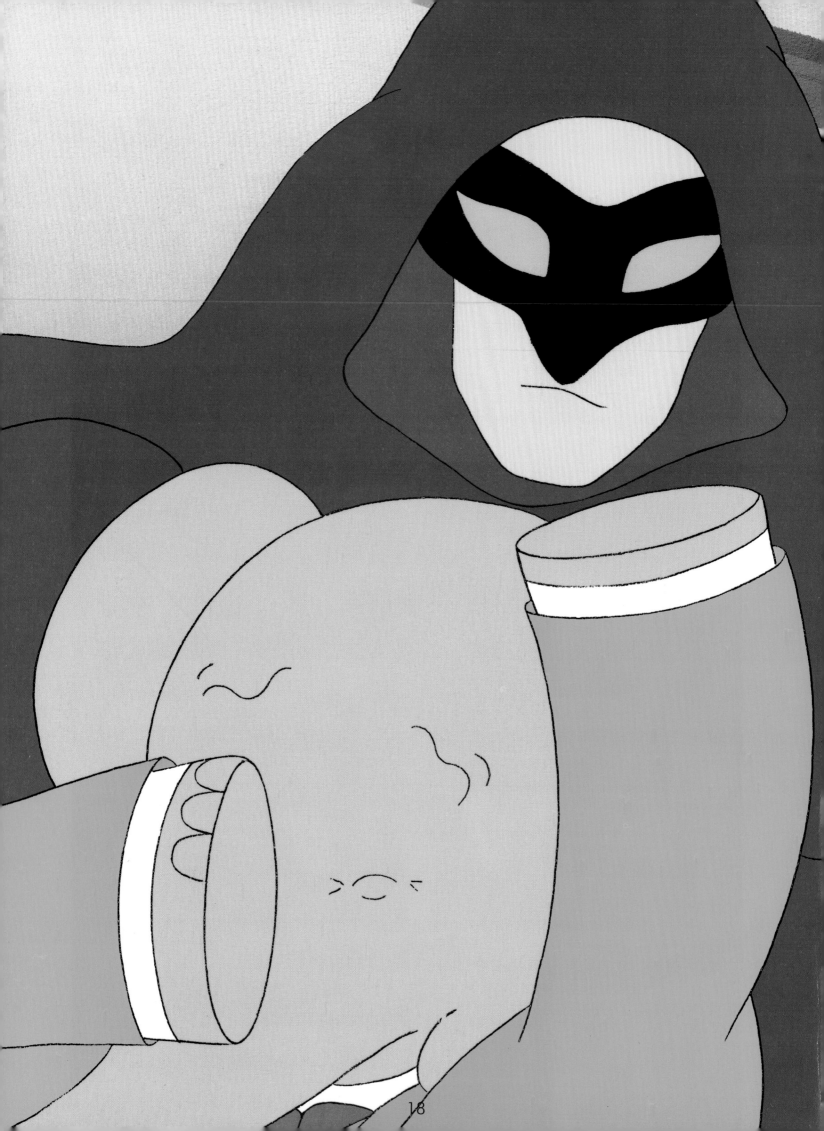

Babar had seen enough. He spun around, but before he could creep out again, the phantom grabbed him by the shoulders.

"Who are you?" he roared in a voice like thunder. It was impossible for Babar to escape, although he squirmed and kicked like a whirlwind.

The phantom held on. But in the struggle, the hood of his cape dropped back, and his mask fell off. The person revealed was no ghost. He was not even frightening. He was just a tall man, with white hair and a sad expression. Babar felt rather sorry for him. What could have happened to make this man disguise himself and hide in a deserted building? Babar didn't understand, but he wanted to. In the meantime, he held out his hand and said, "My name is Babar. How do you do?"

The phantom shook hands, and without giving his name, began to tell his story.

"It was here, in this town, many years ago, that everything began," the phantom told Babar. "I met a beautiful young girl who believed in me and my musical talent. The first time she heard me play, she told me I was truly gifted and belonged on the concert stage. However, she said I should study in Austria—in Vienna, the great city of music. She was so sure, and I wanted to please her so much, that one day I left for Austria.

22

"When I arrived in Vienna, instead of working hard, I was lazy and waited for success to come to me. Of course, it never arrived. I was so ashamed that when I returned home, I disguised myself. For many years now, I have pretended to be the phantom of the old opera house. It was the only way to keep people away. And it worked, except for you, Babar," he concluded, smiling softly.

Babar decided that someone should help the phantom rejoin the world and forget his sad past. And it might as well be him.

He started a petition: "Performers, Musicians, Workers, Merchants, Young and Old, Boys and Girls, let's work together to restore the old Opera House!"

At the end of the first day, Babar knew he would succeed. He had collected over a thousand signatures. Several days later he took the petition to the mayor's office. When the mayor saw all the signatures, he made a decision. "Obviously, the people want the opera house restored. Let's do it."

Babar ran to the opera house to give his new friend the good news.

But instead of being happy to return to the world, the musician was furious. "What have you done to me, you meddling little elephant? I only wished to be left alone in peace! Can't you understand that?" And with those words, he left Babar and fled into the deep cellars of the opera house.

In the meantime, the mayor had an architect check over the building. The architect decided that certain parts of it were unsafe, and he would have to take them down before beginning the repairs. The mayor came to the opera house to give the bulldozers the word to start.

The engines had already been turned on when the Old Lady appeared, looking very worried. "Babar has disappeared!" she called to the mayor, at the top of her voice. Unfortunately, the mayor couldn't hear what she said, because of the noise of the machinery.

Babar had been trying to find the phantom's hiding place and warn him.

"They are planning to destroy the opera house," he called out. "If you don't come out, you will be buried under tons of bricks."

When the Old Lady picked her way across the littered stage, she found that Babar had tripped over a rope. It had wrapped itself around his ankle and now he was dangling over the open cellar below the stage. To make matters worse, the staircase had caved in when he tried to catch hold of it!

The Old Lady ran for help immediately.
The mayor stopped the bulldozers and ran in
to try and grab the rope that held Babar. He
and one of the workmen arrived just in time.

Together they hoisted Babar out of the black hole. The little elephant was saved. The Old Lady hugged him and kissed away his tears of relief.

36

Babar was even more thankful when he saw the phantom rushing up to answer his own cries for help. When the phantom saw the Old Lady, he stopped in his tracks. Then she cried out, "You? Here? You are the phantom of the opera house? Tell me I'm not dreaming!"

"You not dreaming, my dear one," answered the phantom. "It is really I." And he added softly, "After all these years you haven't changed."

Then he turned to Babar and said, "Thank you, Babar. Through your kindness, I have found the person who believed in me once . . ."

"Once!" interrupted the Old Lady. "I believed in you then, I believe in you now. When one has genius, it is forever."

She was right. Encouraged, the former phantom began to plan a magnificent concert. His debut at the newly restored opera house was a great success. At last, his brilliant career was underway.

"And that's the end of the story," concluded Babar. "We all need help and encouragement, whether we know it or not. And so, Pom, if Flora is willing to show you how to play the piano, don't send her away."

Pom understood the lesson. But that night it was Babar who played for them, recalling the time when a phantom had kept his talent a secret. This time, the music took wing through the starry night.